For every injustice felt by a parent.

The Variant

Published by Divergent Mind Books

ISBN: 978-1-918145-00-7

50% of the author's net profit from the sale of this book will be donated to The Divergent Mind Books Association, an unincorporated not-for-profit association dedicated to supporting neurodivergent authors.

The Variant

David Peters

Divergent Mind Books

The Muted Sky

The air in Neo-Veridia had the colour of old cement, perpetually shrouded in a haze that seemed to cling to everything. It was an oppressive atmosphere, thick with the stale smell of recycled synthetics that never quite masked the faint, metallic tang of the Authority's silent surveillance network. This was a city where technology and control intertwined seamlessly, creating an environment that felt both suffocating and inescapable.

Kaelen lived on the outskirts of the Recognised Zone, in a forgotten sector where the crumbling buildings towered like ghosts from a bygone era. Here, the only movement came from dust motes swirling lazily in the dim light, a stark contrast to the underlying tension that gripped the community. The subtle, creeping fear instilled by the Social Engineers, the shadowy figures who operated coldly and efficiently on behalf of the Authority, hung over the streets like a heavy fog. Their impassive faces and unyielding directives reminded everyone that they were always being watched, their lives dictated by an ever-present, invisible hand. It was a place where hope felt like a distant memory, always overshadowed by the relentless control of a regime that seemed to grow stronger with each passing day.

He was a Variant, a man whose neural pathways resonated with a different, dissonant tune. This unique neurological configuration granted him an extraordinary ability, an ability that the Authority, in its infinite yet sterile wisdom, deemed a fundamental threat to the stability of its "Harmonious Collective." The Authority, intent on maintaining a seamless, cohesive society, viewed any deviation from their carefully constructed norms with deep suspicion and fear.

Kaelen's ability was not flashy in the traditional sense; it involved neither bursts of fire nor elaborate displays of telekinesis. Instead, his skill lay in a profound perception of the world around him. He could feel the patterns, see, in his mind's eye, the invisible yet intricate web of electromagnetic and psychic energy that interconnected all entities, both living and inorganic. This perception allowed him to anticipate events with uncanny precision. He could sense the exact microsecond when a bridge support would succumb to the relentless forces of nature, or when someone's carefully crafted lie would crack under the strain of their own deception, causing their voice to waver and falter. To Kaelen, these moments were more than mere flashes of insight; they were glimpses into the fundamental truths that underpinned existence. Each revelation filled him with a blend of awe and dread, as he understood the potential for chaos that lay beneath the surface of the Authority's façade of order. To the Authority, however, he represented a significant risk, a walking, breathing flaw in their meticulously controlled design, a reminder that no system could be truly flawless when faced with the unpredictable nature of human potential.

As he navigated a world that sought to suppress his gifts, he remained acutely aware of the thin line he walked between being a harbinger of understanding and an outcast marked for elimination.

The Law, however, stood as an unyielding fortress, cold and inflexible in its principles. It stipulated that no citizen could be openly punished for identifying as a Variant; rather, they could only be monitored. This provision was intended to protect individuals from overt discrimination, yet it also created a chilling atmosphere of surveillance and control. The Authority was aware that this arrangement lacked teeth, without a mechanism for enforcement, compliance could not be guaranteed. As a result, they sought a loophole, a subtle yet effective means to ensure that those who were different remained in line. The challenge was to establish a system that could influence behaviour without overtly violating the Law.

On a particularly chilly evening, the doorbell to his cramped apartment rang, breaking the silence that had settled over the dimly lit room. When he opened the door, he found two black-clad Compliance Officers standing rigidly on his doorstep. Their sombre attire contrasted sharply with the warmth of the home behind him. They didn't arrive with handcuffs or the threat of immediate arrest; rather, they held a meticulously forged legal document that felt heavy with consequence.

The lead officer, a woman with eyes as flat and cold as polished slate, stepped forward, her demeanour devoid of any warmth or empathy. "Your children, Variant Kaelen," she began, her voice steady and unsettling, "are now the subject of an official investigation." She paused, appearing to gather her thoughts as the weight of her words hung heavily in the air. "Your... differences... present a statistically significant and unpredictable risk of detrimental psychological development and potential physical endangerment to Minors Elara and Jorun."

As the implications of her statement settled in, he felt a rush of confusion and fear swell within him. The term "protective custody" echoed in his mind, a bureaucratic phrase that stripped away any sense of security for his family. "They are hereby placed in temporary protective custody," she concluded without a hint of compassion. His heart raced as he struggled to comprehend the meaning of her words. The severity of the situation was overwhelming, and he could feel the walls closing in around him. What did they mean by "risk"? How could they deem him a danger when all he wanted was to provide a loving home for his children? He could only stare at the officers, questions swirling through his mind as a sense of helplessness washed over him. This was not just a bureaucratic decision; this was a life-altering moment that threatened to separate him from the very essence of his being, his children.

Elara, his six-year-old daughter, with her deep-sea blue eyes mirroring his own, was intently clutching a faded star chart. The chart, tattered and worn at the edges, was a remnant of the adventures he had shared with her, filled with constellations and the faint outlines of distant galaxies. Beside her, Jorun, his son, just a year younger, sat on the floor, completely absorbed in his task. He was drawing geometric shapes, squares, triangles, and circles, each one meticulously crafted with a creativity that reminded Kaelen of his own childhood.

Kaelen felt a growing unease settling around him, like a thick fog that obscured everything familiar. The atmosphere seemed to pulse with an urgent energy, vibrating with a tension that was impossible to ignore. It was as if the very fabric of their surroundings was alive, sending out frantic signals that resonated within him, echoing his own inner turmoil. The patterns in the air screamed for his attention, a high-pitched alarm ringing in his ears that tugged at the edges of his consciousness. Deep down, he could sense the alarm's escalating intensity, whispering to him in an urgent tone that he needed to act. Yet, despite this instinctive urging, he found himself paralysed, at a loss for words and action. His tongue felt heavy, as though it were weighed down by the burdens of unspoken fears and distant memories. Each thought weighed heavily on him, and the tension in the pit of his stomach tightened like a vice. His heart raced, pounding against his ribs in response to the silent chaos that brewed just beneath the surface of their once-tranquil setting. On the outside, everything appeared calm, but inwardly, he could feel the storm brewing, dark and foreboding.

5

"Cooperate, citizen Kaelen," hissed the slate-eyed officer standing nearby. Her expression was cold and unyielding as she led the crying children away. "Compliance secures their safety. Resistance leads to... inconvenience." The officer's voice dripped with authority that sent chills down Kaelen's spine. He understood the threat behind her words all too well. His difference, once a source of pride, had become a leash tightening around his neck with every moment they spent in this precarious situation. His children, who once brought him joy, now felt like an anchor pulling him deeper into the murky waters of despair.

In the days that followed, he fought back, invoking every section of the Citizens' Rights Mandate. He shouted the law at them until his throat was raw. But the law was a weapon wielded by the Authority, not against it. They had taken his children and hidden them in the labyrinth of the State's secret facilities, a place he couldn't access or navigate.

Kaelen was torn between the instinct to fight for his children's freedom and the urgent need to protect them at any cost. To ensure their well-being, he soon realised he had to become invisible, like a ghost slipping through the Authority's watchful gaze. His identity had to shift; he needed to blend in and become a perfect, compliant cog in the overwhelming machine that sought to control him. Every decision felt like a careful balance between self-preservation and the desire to stand up against the oppressive forces that threatened to destroy his children.

The stakes were high, and every moment counted in a world where compliance could mean the difference between safety and danger.

The Gavel and the Ghost

The life of a state puppet was a dismal existence, stripped of freedom and fraught with anxiety. Each day was weighed down by the constant fear that one wrong move could lead to insidious punishments for his children, a thought that loomed over him like an ominous cloud. This pervasive fear kept an iron grip on his heart, limiting his actions and binding his spirit. Every morning, he awoke with the knowledge that his choices, however small, bore the potential to impact not only his own life but also the lives of those he loved most dearly.

Now, Kaelen found himself forced to work for the authorities, enduring gruelling shifts at their refinery during the graveyard hours, when the world outside was silent and shadowy. The job was simple yet exhausting: he manually moved heavy carts of refined ore from the massive machine to the trains that waited to transport the ore away, out of Neo-Veridia and across the barren countryside. These trains carried the precious ore through the Dead Valley, a desolate stretch of land that echoed with the stories of those who had come before, and over the border into Middleland. Eventually, the ore would reach the port of Bermial, a place filled with both promise and peril.

As Kaelen performed his labour, he often found himself reflecting on the whispered stories he had heard about the port of Bermial. Tales circulated among the workers, tales of people fleeing to that distant place, making risky deals with unscrupulous captains who would hide stowaways in exchange for a few extra credits or rare gems. Often, these stories painted pictures of desperate souls seeking freedom, slipping away from the oppressive grip of their home. Whenever Kaelen heard such tales, he listened intently, a mix of envy and regret swelling within him. He frequently wished he had made the choice to escape when he still had his children with him, but the past was a realm he could not change.

However, running wouldn't help his children now; he understood that only a profound understanding of the law could offer them any semblance of protection and hope for a better future. So, in the midst of his labour and the weight of his fears, he began to learn. He sought out knowledge, first diving into the digital chronicles written by scholars and experts who offered insights into the complexities of the system that held him captive. With the meagre credits he had managed to scrape together from his arduous work, he enrolled in a distance learning course, eager to equip himself with the knowledge that might someday empower him to fight for his children's rights.

As he delved deeper into legal texts and case studies, Kaelen felt a spark of determination igniting within him. He envisioned a future where he could advocate for those like him, who felt powerless and trapped under the watchful gaze of the state. Each lesson he absorbed was not just an academic exercise but a step toward liberation, not just for himself, but also for his children. With this renewed focus and the flicker of hope in his heart, he pressed on, firm in his resolve that he would not only survive but also strive to create a different reality for his family.

Over the next two years, he worked hard at night and studied harder in the day. His pursuit came at a cost; restful sleep was a rare luxury. When he did manage to close his eyes, he often found himself haunted by dreams that featured Elara's face, her features etched into his memory with vivid clarity. The precise shade of her hair would flash before him, intertwining with the serifs of the legal code that occupied his waking thoughts. Alongside those dreams was the empty space where Jorun's small, warm hand used to fit perfectly in his. This absence left a profound void in the intricate pattern of his soul, reminding him constantly of what he had lost and what he was fighting for. Through it all, Kaelen's determination only grew stronger; he was resolved to turn his grief and frustration into a weapon of its own, aiming to challenge the Authority and reclaim his right to family.

Then, the comm-unit from the Authority, in his pocket, vibrated. It wasn't a court summons; it was a terse, official notification from the Ministry of Child Welfare. Minor Elara Kaelen. Termination of Custody Status. Cause of Death: Advanced Neuro-Atypical Atrophy. Kaelen didn't scream. The pattern around him didn't fracture. It went absolutely, terrifyingly silent. Neuro-Atypical Atrophy, a sterile, jargonistic term for a condition that only seemed to surface in children separated from their Variant parents. It was a lie, a poison, a slow-acting warning. Back off, Kaelen. You are fighting a lie with a greater truth, and we hold the greater truth's cost.

He looked at the small, faded star-chart he still kept. Elara had always wanted to see the real sky, unmuted by Neo-Veridia's haze. She would never see it.

But the death didn't break him; it fused him. The loss was the fuel that burned away the last vestiges of fear and caution. He was no longer fighting to get his children back; he was fighting to avenge his daughter and free his son.

Kaelen doubled his efforts and, within two months, completed his Juris Doctorate with top honours. His thesis, a stunning deconstruction of the 'Future Harm' doctrine, was a legal time bomb. He filed his petition, naming the Ministry, the lead officer, and the entire apparatus of the Compliance Authority. The filing was so technically perfect, so meticulously researched, that the courts, bound by their own procedural law, couldn't

11

dismiss it outright. The Authority couldn't afford and sought to avoid a public trial. A full legal battle would expose their methods, their institutionalised discrimination. They preferred their power to be a silent weight, not a loud confrontation. They blinked. Not in surrender, but in a tactical retreat. Kaelen was summoned not to a courtroom, but to a pristine, white-walled chamber for a "Mandatory Parental Reassessment and Demonstration of Rehabilitative Compliance."

The panel was three high-ranking officials, including a visibly uncomfortable, ageing judge, called Aemes whom, through his study, Kaelen knew had a shred of integrity left.

"Variant Kaelen," the slate-eyed officer, now a Director, began, her voice smooth as oil. "The Authority acknowledges your exemplary efforts in seeking mainstream accreditation and your demonstrated commitment to the Collective's standards. Due to an unforeseen procedural review, we are compelled to officially reassess your suitability as a parent to Minor Jorun Kaelen."

It was a performance, a meticulous piece of legal theatre. Kaelen knew the drill. He was to perform a father's humility, a citizen's repentance, and a Variants subservience. He answered their questions with the cold, precise language of the Law, never slipping into emotion. Yes, he understood the importance of social uniformity. Yes, he agreed that his unique traits should be managed. Yes, he would ensure Jorun was thoroughly shielded from any 'non-Collective' influences. He was a master actor now, wearing the mask of perfect conformity. He had to be. Jorun was still breathing, still hidden.

The Director smiled, a thin, chilling curve of the lips. "Very well. The panel finds that you have shown adequate steps toward rehabilitation and compliance, and that, pending ongoing bi-weekly review, Minor Jorun Kaelen may be considered for a phased return to your custody." The judge nodded, relief plain on his tired face. Kaelen had won a battle, an inch of ground in the Authority's fortress.

But Kaelen didn't celebrate. He felt the pattern of the room, the Director's triumphant smirk, the panel's manufactured relief. He knew the reassessment was tripe, an administrative sleight-of-hand. They hadn't validated him as a father; they had simply decided that, with one child already dead and the other's fate still in their hands, Kaelen was a more manageable threat outside the courts, under their constant, suffocating watch.

He stood, the perfect, reformed citizen. His eyes, the colour of a dead sea, met the Director's. "I accept the decision," he stated, his voice flat. "But Director, I remind you that I retain full legal standing to petition for damages related to the death of Minor Elara Kaelen."

He wasn't bowing down; he was simply changing his vantage point. He had his degree, he had his vengeance, and soon, he would have his son.

The Return and the Last Train

The agenda clearly stated that Joren, his son, would be brought to their residence at ten in the morning. As the clock ticked towards that hour, anticipation surged within Kaelen. At five past ten, he found himself standing in the doorway of his flat, peering intently down the ochre-misted road. The air was thick with pollution, but he strained to discern any sign of his son through the haze that blurred the lines of the familiar surroundings.

Kaelen's heart raced as he thought about the moment they would finally reunite. Although he felt hopeful, a part of him struggled to fully believe that this long-awaited reunion was actually happening. Memories of the time they had spent apart flooded his mind, each one a reminder of the love and connection they once shared. Standing there, he felt his heart dance delicately inside his chest, each beat echoing the nervous excitement coursing through him.

As he continued to watch, the outlines of figures began to materialise in the distance, gradually becoming clearer as they approached. Kaelen's breath caught in his throat; anticipation mingled with anxiety. Would Joren recognise him? Would they still be close, or would it merely be the beginning of another complicated chapter in their lives? With so many questions swirling in his mind, he stayed rooted in place, eager yet apprehensive, waiting for the moment that would change everything...

He returned to his apartment, his mind racing as he tried to project an air of calm and control, determined not to appear desperate. He paced for a while, glancing at the clock as seconds stretched into what felt like eternity. Finally, a knock at the door jolted him from his thoughts. Taking a deliberate moment to collect himself, he opened the door to find two Social Engineers standing there, their expressions barely contained as they forced back smiles on their pale faces. He immediately noted the absence of Joren, his heart sinking with apprehension.

"We regret to inform you that there has been an unexpected development, which means Joren cannot return to your care today," said the taller woman, her tone laced with a feigned concern that only heightened his unease. Instantly, he sensed the machinations at play; this was the Authority messing with him, and he knew this would be just the beginning of his troubles. The implications of her words hung heavy in the air, filling him with dread. Without revealing the cracks threatening to appear in his fragile heart, he maintained his composure and asked, "I see. What exactly is the delay?"

The smaller woman shot him a dark glare, her irritation palpable as she seemed annoyed by his lack of distress. "There has been an issue with power outages at Computer Central, which is slowing down transfers!"

she snapped, as if that would elicit a reaction of despair from him.

Remaining calmer than ever, fully aware that his composed demeanour would only serve to infuriate them further, he replied with a measured tone, "Thank you for taking the time to visit and inform me. Would you like to come in for a refreshment after your journey here?"

That surely struck a nerve; their eyes gleamed with disdain at his unexpected hospitality. They politely refused, their expressions hardening, and then turned to leave, their disappointment evident. Kaelen closed the door behind them, a heavy silence enveloping him as the world paused for a moment, for the collecting of his thoughts, but it was futile. He sank down to the floor against the door, the composed facade he had managed to maintain crumbled, giving way to a wave of emotion. Tears streamed down his face as he grappled with the overwhelming sense of loss and uncertainty that had taken hold of him. Each sob echoed in the empty space, underscoring his feelings of isolation and despair as he wondered what this latest twist meant for his future and Joren's fate.

Stillness enveloped his mind and body as he sat with his back against the door. He remained there, frozen in thought, as the dark shadows of evening began to fill his apartment.

Suddenly, the work alarm jolted him into action. He collected his lunchbox and flask, put on his jacket, and left the flat. With unwavering determination, he walked down the dimly lit street towards the refinery where he would begin his shift. The rhythmic sound of his boots against the pavement echoed in the quiet evening air, mingling with the distant hum of machinery coming to life. As he passed through the underpass, a familiar and unsettling scene greeted him: beggars and hybrid outcasts huddled against the cold, damp walls, all desperately seeking shelter from the biting northerly winds that swept in with the dusk.

Among them, he could see many Variants, individuals who bore the marks of a society that had cast them aside. Their faces were lined with hardship, and their eyes reflected the same twisted, painful truths that Kaelen felt deep within his own heart. It was a painful reminder of his own struggle and the isolation that came with being different in a world that valued conformity. Every glance exchanged with those suffering souls resonated with an unspoken understanding, a silent acknowledgement of their shared plight. In that moment, Kaelen was acutely aware of the cruel reality that enveloped Neo-Veridia: there was no place for Variants in this city governed by rigid norms and unforgiving expectations. It was a truth that hung heavily in the air, one that he felt he could no longer accept. With each step, he felt an increasing urgency to escape the confines of a life that seemed destined to suffocate anyone who dared to deviate from the norm. He knew he had to get away…

The shift took on a different rhythm than the previous ones he had experienced. Tonight, he was not just going through the motions of his work; he was fully engaged, applying himself with an intensity fuelled by a deep sense of purpose. His eyes were wide open, scanning the surroundings intently, searching for any opportunity to gain an advantage that might allow him to escape the confines of his dreary existence.

The old tales of people escaping to the port of Bermial echoed in his mind as he toiled away. Those stories of daring escapes and newfound freedoms powered his imagination. How did they manage to slip away unnoticed? What clever tricks did they employ to conceal their movements from the watchful eyes of authority?

As he filled cart after cart with refined ore, he kept a vigilant gaze on the train, hoping to find hidden spaces where someone could potentially hide. There had to be a nook or cranny somewhere that could serve as a refuge for those seeking to flee, unless, of course, those enchanting stories were merely fabrications woven from desperate dreams. A wave of sadness washed over him at the thought that the only hint of a way out from the harsh reality of Neo-Veridia might be nothing more than a fantasy. What if the only hope he clung to was just a mirage in the desert of his reality? He shook his head to dispel the thoughts, determined to keep searching, to stay focused. After all, someone had to uncover the truth behind those stories, and perhaps that someone could be him. As he worked, he felt the weight of his dreams pressing down on him, urging him not to give up. The night was long, and as the shadows stretched across the ground, he promised himself that he would keep looking for a glimmer of hope amidst the darkness.

The hours wore on, and tonight's enthusiasm began to take its toll as he struggled more and more with the heavy unloading. Finally, it became overwhelming. As he shovelled a load of ore into one of the train's carts, he fell forward, face-first into the ore. In that moment, fate took a turn for Kaelen. When his shovel struck the carriage's floor, it made a softer, hollow sound instead of the solid thud he expected. Synapses fired in his mind, and he instantly realised that fate had delivered him an answer: the bottom of this carriage was hollow. This was how he could escape with Joren. No one would suspect anyone was hidden beneath tons of refined ore. Now the only question was how to access the smuggling hold below. Getting to his feet, he looked around, checking for any guard or worker watching.

No one was around, and Kaelen suddenly realised it was breaktime. Taking advantage of the moment, he quickly crawled under the carriage, his heart racing with anticipation. In the dim light, he discovered a door leading to the secret hold, a place that promised escape. A brief look around confirmed that the hold was spacious enough for three people, though realistically, it would just be him and Joren who would fit snugly, along with a few essential supplies.

With a sense of urgency, Kaelen crawled back out from beneath the carriage and returned to his post, making sure to act nonchalant so no one would notice anything amiss. He made a mental note of the carriage number, knowing that it was their ticket out of this place. The next step in his plan was to find out when that carriage would be utilised again, as timing was crucial.

As the night wore on, he formulated his strategy. Toward the end of his shift, he deliberately forced his shovel between two sleepers, exerting enough pressure for the handle to snap off. It was a calculated move, as it meant he would have to report to the office to fill out an official damage report for the broken tool. Although the cost of a new shovel would be deducted from his credits, a financial blow he could ill afford, he didn't care. What truly mattered was having a legitimate reason to be in the office, where the transport reports were kept and where he could gather critical information.

When the clerk left the room to fetch another shovel from the equipment room at the far end of the building, Kaelen seized the opportunity. Employing his photographic memory, he quickly scanned the transport schedules displayed on the wall, noting the movements of that particular carriage. To his relief, he discovered it was scheduled to be used five more times that week. However, there was a catch: after those uses, the carriage would be sent to central for routine maintenance. That was a significant issue because routine maintenance meant that the secret hold would likely be discovered, jeopardising everything they had planned. Now, with a sense of urgency, Kaelen established his deadline: next Friday would be the last train out for him and Joren. Time was running short, and he needed to meticulously figure out how to sneak Joren into the refinery and into the hold without raising any alarms. This required a lot of careful planning. Kaelen had to sign in and out for every shift; in fact, it was only during those moments that he encountered any security personnel. It seemed the refinery's logic dictated that if everyone were monitored upon entry and exit, there was no need to waste resources on constant surveillance. With this in mind, Kaelen pondered the best ways to orchestrate Joren's entry. He knew they would need to avoid drawing attention to themselves, especially during the busier times when security was more vigilant. Perhaps he could create a distraction or find a way to time their movements so that Joren could slip in unnoticed. Each plan would need to be carefully crafted, and every scenario analysed. He couldn't afford to make a single mistake.

The fear of getting caught weighed heavily on his mind, but the thought of freedom spurred him on. Soon, he would be reunited with Joren, then, in that hidden hold, together they could finally escape the confines of Neo-Veridia and the grip it had on their lives. As he worked through the details, Kaelen remained resolute, driven by the hope of a brighter future beyond the looming walls of their current reality.

The Beggar

Kaelen stood at the threshold of his modest home, heart pounding in anticipation. The last time he had seen his son, the boy had been swallowed by the chaos of Neo-Veridia, a place drenched in the sinister shadows of industrial decay. When he finally caught sight of the figures approaching, he strained to recognise his son's familiar silhouette. The social engineers, with their sterile uniforms and emotionless faces, escorted the boy as if he were a fragile piece of glass. His stomach twisted as he noted the way his son's shoulders were hunched, his nervous eyes darting to the ground, avoiding the piercing gazes of the engineers. Their presence felt ominous, as if they were nothing but a cruel reminder of the world the boy had returned from.

As the social engineers completed their cold assessment and prepared to depart, the tension in the air broke. Kaelen rushed to wrap his arms around his son, pulling him into a tight embrace that was both a shield against the harshness of Neo-Veridia and a declaration of unwavering love. In that moment, the boy's facade cracked; he let out a breath he seemed to have been holding since the day he left. Kaelen could feel the shudder that coursed through him as he stepped back, relief washing over them both as the engineers melted into the horizon, like ghosts retreating back into the shadows of a toxic landscape. With every passing second, the oppressive weight of his son's anxiety lifted, replaced by a warmth only home could provide, a sanctuary from the nightmares that flickered at the edges of his mind.

Yet, as night fell over the dystopian skyline, the boy's joy was overshadowed by an unshakable fear that lingered in the corners of his heart. Neo-Veridia was a monument to despair, steel towers loomed like jagged teeth against the darkened sky, and the air was thick with the acrid stench of pollution, choked with the remnants of despairing dreams. He could still hear the cacophony of machinery and distant sirens, feeling the very ground pulse with the frenetic energy of a city that devoured hope. For every moment spent at home, he felt the gnawing reality that he was tethered to a place where humanity slumbered under a heavy blanket of smog. He feared that the moment he stepped back outside, the suffocating grip of Neo-Veridia would close around him once more, entrenching him in a world where innocence struggled to survive.

In the quiet moments when the shadows stretch long and the air thickens with impending gloom, his father's departure felt like a foreboding omen. The echoes of laughter from the day faded, replaced by the oppressive weight of anxiety. Each evening ignited a flicker of dread within him, as he was only too aware of the dark figures that prowled the corners of their existence, the Social Engineers, entities that stalked the hopeful and the broken alike. His memories of the orphanage spun into focus, vivid and haunting. The stench of decay and despair clung to the damp walls, wrapping around him like a suffocating shroud. He could almost hear the flickering fluorescent lights buzzing overhead, toying with his mind as he lay curled on the unforgiving cot. Every corner echoed with the cries of the lost and the abandoned; whispers of children who had long since learned that hope was a fleeting luxury.

It was there, in that wretched place, that he had lost not just his childhood, but also his sister, the only glimmer of warmth in an otherwise barren landscape. The day they took her away felt like the earth beneath him shifted, leaving him stranded in a void. He remembered the way she had clung to him, eyes wide with fear, as the cold hands of the staff pried them apart. "I'll come back for you," she had promised, her voice trembling, yet filled with a fierce resolve. But promises were meaningless in the orphanage, a place where hope was systematically crushed.

Her absence became a gaping wound in his soul, a constant reminder that belonging was a cruel illusion. With her gone, the will to survive dwindled, leaving behind a hollow husk. Nights grew unbearable; sleep turned into a restless battleground where he fought against the echoes of her laughter and his own despair. The other children, consumed by their own darkness, became mere shadows, faces that blurred together in a sea of sorrow. He learned to navigate the landscape of cruelty alone, recoiling from the taunts of the guards who revelled in the misery they inflicted.

Each day had melded into the next, punctuated only by the harsh clang of metal doors and the distant wails of children succumbing to hopelessness. The meagre meals were often cold, just like the hearts of those who administered them, and every bite felt like a betrayal of his sister's memory. He was left to languish in a world where kindness was an alien concept, where the glimmer of companionship flickered and faded like a dimming star.

And now, as he faced the impending return of the very forces that had shattered his world, the fear gnawed at him like a relentless beast. Would he be forced back into that living nightmare? The thought coiled around his heart, threatening to strangle any remnants of hope he clung to. The City's orphanage loomed in his mind like a spectre, and the thought of being severed from the fleeting kindness his father provided ignited a primal fear within him. The fragility of his existence was not lost on him; in a world designed to break the spirit of those like him, he fought fiercely to retain the memories of his sister, the light that once illuminated his darkest corners, even as the chilling shadows threatened to engulf him once more. He held his sister's toy close to his heart, the wood was worn and smoothed by touch, a testament to countless moments of laughter and shared dreams. It symbolised not only her childhood innocence but also the indelible mark she left on his life. As he felt the familiar contours of the toy, a wave of warmth washed over him, mixed with the bittersweet ache of loss. Memories flooded his mind: her infectious laughter, the way her eyes sparkled with joy, and the countless adventures they had in the backyard, where imagination knew no bounds.

A deep calm fell over him, yet it was tinged with urgency. He realised, as the weight of his thoughts settled in, that he could not remain in the suffocating grip of Neo-Veridia any longer. The oppressive walls felt like they were closing in, a stark reminder of his sister's absence and the relentless danger surrounding them. He needed to escape, not just for himself, but for his dad too, who had been silently fighting his own battles since they lost her.

The thought of freeing both of them from this place filled him with a sense of purpose. He envisioned a future where they could create new memories, a future where his sister's spirit could live on in their laughter, unburdened by the shadows of their past. Summoning every ounce of courage, Joren tightened his grip on the toy, making a silent promise. He would find a way out of Neo-Veridia, even if it meant standing against the odds. Together, they would reclaim their lives, honour her memory, and find the light again.

As Kaelen made his way to work, a beggar suddenly collapsed in front of him. Seeing this, he decided to help the beggar, giving him some of his food and a few credits. Grateful, the beggar expressed his indebtedness and mentioned that he had been observing Kaelen at work. Staring at him with an understanding expression, the man spoke, "I knew it the moment I saw your eyes yesterday! I recognise the pain you try to hide. That pain is my only companion these days, for I once stood where you stand now. I tell you, I wish I had made the choice you are making." He revealed that he used to work in the refinery as well and was aware of Kaelen's secret plan to escape. "You will need oxygen to breathe as the train runs through the valley. I can source that for you!"

Kaelen realised he hadn't even considered the consequences of travelling through Dead Valley, where the pollution was so severe that nothing could survive. He froze in place as it dawned on him that his actions could have led to not only his own death but also the death of his beloved son.

The beggar recognised the look on Kaelen's face. "You aren't the first to try to escape, and you won't be the last! Many have perished crossing it, which is why I watch—I look for those few who are brave enough to try! I salute you, for it's something I failed to do!" He admitted that he was too scared to escape himself and had seen his family destroyed because of it. "You will get out," he assured Kaelen, "with my help!"

As the two men spoke, the air around them grew heavy with the scent of rain mingled with the acrid odour of pollution. The dark clouds above rumbled ominously, releasing a constant drizzle that fell in lazy sheets, each drop dirtying the cobblestones beneath their feet. The city wore a muted palette of greys and browns, a reminder of the toxic factories lining the horizon. Kaelen pulled the collar of his worn coat closer to his throat, feeling the chill seep in. The rain stung against his skin, each droplet carrying with it the sharp, metallic tang of contamination.

"Listen closely," the beggar murmured, his voice barely rising above the patter of the rain. He leaned closer, his breath warm against Kaelen's ear, though it did little to quell the chill hanging in the air. The beggar's face was shadowed, his features defined by the dim light of a flickering streetlamp. "The secret entrance is hidden behind the old loading bay. When you sign out for the night, meet me here, I will have the oxygen you will need!"

Kaelen narrowed his eyes, nodding slowly, trying to piece together the beggar's words. "And after I get inside, how do I make it to the smuggler's hold?" His voice was laced with a mixture of scepticism and hope, like the tangled remnants of a once vibrant web now reduced to frayed threads.

"There's a service tunnel that runs beneath the main floor," the beggar replied, his gaze unwavering. "It's dark and narrow, but the air is less toxic down there. Just keep your wits about you. You'll enter near the back; that's where they unload shipments. From there, it's just a matter of timing."

Kaelen nodded again, his heart racing at the prospect of freedom, a life where he wouldn't have to hide his or his son's true nature. "I… I need to ensure Joren, my son, is safe," he stammered, unease creeping into his tone. "Can I trust you with him?" To reassure him, the beggar rolled up the sleeve of his ragged coat, revealing a faded tattoo, a poignant reminder of a past etched into his skin. Its once-bright colours were now muted under layers of grime, but the symbol remained distinct: the emblem of heroes from the old resistance. "I am not just a beggar. My name is Eldric; I fought for justice once. I will protect your son as if he were my own flesh and blood." This revelation washed over Kaelen like the polluted rain streaming down from the sky. Here stood a man who carried the weight of revolution on his skin, a remnant of hope in this dreary place. He took a deep breath, swallowing the fear that threatened to engulf him. "Thank you," he said finally, determination swelling in his chest. "I'll trust you."

As they spoke, the rain intensified, a heavy downpour that sounded more like an ominous drumroll than a gentle shower. Each drop splashed against the ground with a force that sent up small puffs of mud, mingling with the viscous liquid already pooled at their feet. Flashes of lightning illuminated their surroundings, casting fleeting shadows across the beggar's face, showcasing the lines of struggle etched there. Kaelen shivered as the electric air vibrated around them, a reminder of the storm brewing both outside and within his heart.

"Meet me back here at midnight on Friday," the beggar instructed, his voice firm yet compassionate. "I'll have Joren, and then, after you finish, you both will begin your journey." With one last penetrating look, he turned, disappearing into the shadows of the alley. Kaelen watched him go, the cold rain now soaking through his clothes as anxiety twisted in his gut.

With Friday night's plan set in motion, Kaelen felt the weight of his decision settling in. He had chosen a path fraught with uncertainty, but for the sake of his son, he would brave whatever dangers awaited them both in the darkened corridors of the refinery. The poisoned rain continued to drench the city, but in his heart, a flicker of hope ignited, promising a chance for freedom against the oppressive grip of despair.

A Child's Fears

Once Kaelen stepped through the door, fatigue washed over him as he was greeted by Joren's wide eyes and an exuberant grin. The relief that Joren felt to see his father home safely was palpable, almost tangible in the air between them. Kaelen smiled back, his heart heavy from the day's burdens but lifted by his son's presence. "Hey there, champ," Kaelen said softly, his voice warm despite the weariness lining his face. He walked across the room, shedding his heavy boots with a sigh of relief. The familiar ritual welcomed him home: the clatter of boots hitting the floor, the gentle easing of tired muscles as he slipped into the comfort of his slippers.

"Did you finish your colouring?" he asked, throwing a glance at the digital screen where colourful shapes danced under Joren's nimble fingers, a creative escape from the harsh realities of their world.

"Almost! Look, this is the dragon I made!" Joren said, excitement bubbling as he pointed to a vibrant dragon swirling around in shades of blue and green. "That looks fantastic," Kaelen replied, settling into his worn armchair with a drink in hand, allowing the cool liquid to wash over him and spread a momentary comfort through his tired body. They shared a quiet moment, the kind that came so easily between them, but soon

Joren's brows knitted in concern, breaking the peaceful silence.

"Dad," he started, his voice dipping, "do you ever think about... escaping?" Joren, eyes flickering with uncertainty, continued, "I don't feel we're safe here. What if they come back for us? What if I lose you like I lost her?" The words came tumbling out, weighty with fear and grief, tangled together like thorns in his chest. Kaelen listened intently, letting Joren voice the thoughts he'd been harbouring. He allowed silence to settle, knowing that sometimes, just being there was what his son needed most.

"I think about it all the time," Joren continued, his tone trembling, "I feel like we're living in a cage. Just waiting for the moment when it all falls apart again." He glanced down, his fingers momentarily pausing on the screen. "What if we disappear... What if we just... ran away? Somewhere far away, where we can finally be free. Away from all of this." Joren's breath quickened as his mind painted pictures of distant places, filled with lush, untouched landscapes where the shadows of the past could never reach them. "What if they come for us, Dad? What if they take you this time?" His voice dipped to a whisper, trembling with the weight of potential loss. Kaelen's heart twisted painfully as he watched his son reveal the depths of his anxiety. The memories of his daughter, lost to the chaos that once consumed their lives, rose unbidden to his thoughts. "I don't want to lose you, too," Joren finished, his voice barely above a whisper.

Kaelen's silence stretched, a comforting presence amid the storm of Joren's fears, as he soaked in the rawness of his son's emotions. For a moment, he felt the weight of the world pressing against his ribs, an invisible burden that had grown heavier since their lives had been turned upside down. Finally, leaning forward in his armchair, Kaelen broke the silence. "Joren," he began, his voice steady despite the gravity of their conversation. "You're not alone in this. I feel afraid too, but we've faced so much already." He paused, watching as Joren's eyes searched for reassurance, a lifeline amidst the swell of fear. "But…" Kaelen drew in a deep breath, drawing strength from the love he felt for his son. "…I agree with you."

Joren's gaze snapped up, eyes wide and hopeful. "You do?"

"Yeah," he affirmed softly. "And what's more…" Kaelen leaned closer, his tone shifting to something conspiratorial, "I know how we can escape this city."

Joren blinked in surprise, a mix of disbelief and dawning hope shining in his expression. The weight of the fears they had just shared hung in the air, but it was now accompanied by a flickering light of possibility. "How?" he breathed, leaning forward, his heart racing at the thought of a plan unfurling before him. Kaelen smiled faintly, knowing the journey ahead would be filled with its own challenges, but within this moment, there was a spark of something beautiful: a chance for freedom, a chance for hope.

"Don't worry about the how, just be ready to do what I say, when I say! We are leaving Friday night, but no one must know, and it will be a hard journey. But it's the only way." Joren nodded in obedience, his heart pounding with a mix of excitement and fear. He gazed into his father's eyes, searching for reassurance, knowing that he would do whatever was needed to stay safe and be with him. This moment felt monumental, a pivotal point in their lives where nothing could ever be the same again. As Joren listened to his father's directive, a whirlwind of questions churned in his mind. Why the secrecy? What lay ahead on this journey? But he also felt a deep-seated trust in his dad, who had always protected him, always put his needs first. He had been taught that answers sometimes came at a price, and today was no different.

That was the last time they spoke about the plan. The weight of silence settled between them, leaving Joren in a haze of uncertainty. Was it truly wise to leap into the unknown? Though he wanted to ask about the details, he forced himself to remember what his father had taught him: it was better to remain silent and safe than to risk danger by divulging information that could compromise their escape. After all, the Social Engineers were cunning and invasive, conducting their daily inspections with an intensity that made Joren's skin crawl. He couldn't afford to let slip even the smallest hint of their intentions.

As days dragged on, Joren's thoughts danced between fear and hope. He imagined what their new life might look like, free from the constraints of watchful eyes. He envisioned nights under a blanket of stars, laughing without worry, and exploring life beyond the walls that confined them. Yet the shadows of doubt loomed large as each passing moment brought him closer to the impending departure. Could they truly slip away without a trace? Even amidst his inner turmoil, Joren's determination solidified. He knew his father had a plan, one that might lead them to safety and freedom, and he was resolute in following his lead.

As they prepared for the journey ahead, Joren took a deep breath, steeling himself for whatever lay beyond the dark horizon. He would trust in his father's instincts, keeping the secret locked away, knowing that sometimes, not knowing the how was the best way to ensure their survival…

The Day

Friday night came around quickly, and after a final meal, they both got dressed in warm clothing, ready for their journey. They had packed a rucksack of clothes, food, drink and a few mementoes, they couldn't leave behind. It sat proudly on the table in the living room as they both looked toward it. This was it; there would be no turning back now. They were risking everything for the hope of a better life, and they both knew it. Kaelen approached the rucksack and picked it up, swinging it onto his back. Taking an under-spoken glance towards Joren, he asked, "All set?" Joren nodded, and his father joined in with the nod, took a deep breath and then made for the door.

Just then, as Kaelen reached for the door handle, there was a knock from the other side of the door. He turned to look at Joren and saw the fear in his eyes as he anticipated an end to their world. Turning back to the door, he opened it, finding a male Social Engineer stood there!

"Good evening, I'm Officer Lopez, just here to do the standard daily visit, I hope you don't mind!" the worker said. "But today's visit has already been done, there must be some mistake?" "No, sir, no mistake, you see, we perform spontaneous visits from time to time, to ensure the safety of minors returned to parents' care. May I come in?" Fear struck Kaelen's heart, for if he let the Engineer in, then he would know something was amiss as soon as he saw Joren dressed up, ready for an arduous journey. Behind the door, he waved to Joren to hide, and his son ran to his room silently.

He slowly opened the door, giving Joren extra time to hide. "You must excuse me, officer. I was just on my way to work, and you startled me somewhat when you knocked on the door," he offered as a distracting excuse for his bluntness.

"I excuse nothing and report everything!", the Engineer said as he entered the flat. He was clearly an excellent Social Engineer, cold of heart and completely loyal to the system that mistreated Variants and their families. The man walked about the room, taking note of everything, or at least it seemed so. Kaelen prayed he didn't notice the subtle missing items, like the void on the wall, where the photo-viewer had previously hung.

"So, how is life going with your son home? Are there any difficulties we should know about?" the officer asked.

"No, no difficulties at all. It has been a pleasure having him home, and Joren is very happy and progressing well with his digital education online!" "I have seen his record of education, and it appears somewhat normal, below par, but normal!" the officer continued, trying his hardest to offend Kaelen's sensibilities, trying to make him slip up.

"He has only been home a few days; I am sure he will do better in time. I will work harder with him." The officer was not impressed. "I am sure you will. So, where is Joren then?" he inquired, looking at Kaelen with an argumentative inflexion on his face. "He is in bed, of course. He goes to bed before I leave for work and then gets up after I return home." This was not news and indeed part of the care plan agreed upon, but the officer was there to stir things up and cause a problem, not for any other reason. "That would mean that Joren is home alone during the majority of the night, then, is that right?", "Yes, sir, that is right", answered Kaelen, who was really starting to get concerned at this point.

"Surely, that is not a beneficial situation for young Joren then?" questioned the Officer, confirming his fears. This Engineer was here to make life difficult and possibly remove Joren.

"But sir, it has been agreed, as part of Joren's care plan, that he can be alone at night whilst I work!" "I highly doubt that. Where is the paperwork?" demanded the Officer. He put down his rucksack and headed over to the desk, promptly retrieving a digital reader and pulling up the document on return, before handing it to the Officer, who studied the document for what seemed a lifetime.

"This document is signed by High-Chancellor Judge Aemes, himself. I hope you realise how lucky you are to be granted the High Chancellor's attention!", "Yes, sir, indeed, sir. We are very fortunate!"

"Indeed, you should be.", said the deflated Engineer, who knew too well he couldn't argue against specifications in a document signed from above. "Very well, I will bid you goodnight, " he said, and he started moving towards the door to leave. Just then, the rucksack Kaelen had put down rolled over to one side, and Joren's small hat flopped out onto the floor. Instantly, the atmosphere in the room changed as the officer's eyes looked down at the hat and then back at Kaelen. There was no question, the officer knew something was afoot, and he moved his hand towards his communicator, and that was when Kaelen lost control. He flew at the Officer with a fury he never knew he had, punching him hard and breaking his nose. The officer fought back desperately and landed a couple of blows. As the confrontation escalated, Officer Lopez's hand instinctively moved to his side, swiftly drawing his sonic-driver weapon, aiming it at Kaelen with a hardened glare. In a split second, Kaelen reacted, his adrenaline surging. With a fierce determination, he lunged forward and knocked the weapon out of the officer's hand, sending it clattering to the ground. They grappled in a frenzy, exchanging blows in a chaotic dance of desperation. The officer, trained and skilled, quickly gained the upper hand, delivering a series of punishing strikes. Kaelen fought back with every ounce of strength he had, but it was clear the officer was outmatching him. With a sudden, forceful shove, the officer sent Kaelen sprawling to the ground, breathless and vulnerable.

Kaelen braced himself, feeling the weight of impending doom as the officer loomed over him, fists raised for a deadly strike. Just as the officer readied to deliver the finishing blow, a sharp, echoing sound pierced the tense air, the unmistakable discharge of a sonic-driver.

The officer's eyes widened in surprise as he crumpled to the side, dropping lifelessly to the ground. Kaelen could hardly process what had just happened, his heart racing. He turned to see Joren standing there, his small frame trembling but resolute, gripping the weapon tightly. "Joren…" Kaelen breathed, a mix of relief and shock flooding through him. His son had just killed to save him. In that harrowing moment, everything else faded away; all he could see was the determination in Joren's eyes, a reflection of their shared fight for survival. He stood there in silence, staring at the officer. "What have I done?" he asked. His dad took the weapon from his trembling hands and hugged him tightly. "You did what you had to do…" Kaelen paused, and they both stood there in silence, fully aware that there had been no choice but to act.

"Will they find him?" Joren asked, his voice barely above a whisper, the weight of their secret hanging heavily in the air.

"Yes, they will," Kaelen replied, his brow furrowing as he paused, deep in thought. "But they won't find him here!" With a burst of determination, he dashed into his bedroom, emerging moments later with an old, partially unrolled carpet. It was worn and faded, bearing the marks of time and neglect, but it was just large enough to conceal the officer's body.

With practised efficiency from months of shifting heavy ore, he manoeuvred the lifeless form onto the carpet, rolling it carefully around him. He tied it off with some sturdy knots, ensuring that the body was securely wrapped. The once-unassuming roll of carpet now held a dark secret; all that remained was the ominous bundle, deceptive in its appearance.

Kaelen quickly retrieved a trolley and balanced the rolled carpet upright on it, strapping it in place with more ties. Taking a deep breath, he turned to Joren, a serious glint in his eye. "I'll take this down to the east canal. Stay here and don't let anyone in. I'll be back." With that, he stepped out into the night, the burden of his decision weighing heavily on his shoulders.

The journey to the east canal was a grim affair. As Kaelen wheeled the trolley through the narrow, dimly lit streets, a thick layer of smog hung in the air, wrapping around him like a shroud. The world outside was muted, and shadows danced in and out of focus as he manoeuvred the heavy load. Each breath he took felt acrid, the pollution stinging his lungs as he passed derelict buildings and flickering streetlights. The faint sounds of the city, distant voices, rustling litter, and the low hum of traffic were dulled by the fog, creating an eerie silence that filled him with unease.

As he approached the canal, the scene changed dramatically. The water drifted sluggishly beneath the low-hanging clouds, reflecting the sickly glow of the streetlights above. The smog swirled lazily over the surface of the water, curling and twisting as if trying to hide whatever lay beneath. Kaelen stopped for a moment, feeling the weight of the carpet on the trolley and the gravity of his actions. The canal's surface rippled slightly, disturbed by a light breeze, causing grey tendrils of mist to eddy and swirl. It was in this ghostly environment that the carpet seemed to belong, a part of the darkness that enveloped the area. He glanced around, ensuring he was alone, then released the trolley, carpet and the officer's body, as one, into the murky waters. The moment the fabric met the water, it sank slightly, the dark waves lapping around it as if welcoming it into the depths. Kaelen watched in silence, the smog swirling around him, enveloping the scene as the officer's form disappeared from view.

The fog thickened, obscuring everything around him, and soon, all that was left was a faint ripple in the water, swallowed by the gloomy haze. The officer, whose life was once filled with a despicable purpose, now became just another secret lost to the depths, hidden, forgotten, and forever entwined with the smog that cloaked the city.

With a heavy heart, Kaelen stood, his breath hitching in his throat, and then turned away from the canal. He headed back through the streets, feeling an uncanny sense of finality settle upon him. The air was still thick with smog, but he found a strange solace in knowing that the officer's presence had been erased, at least for now.

First Steps

Joren sat against the far wall, his small figure hunched and trembling as if he were trying to shrink away from the enormity of what had just happened. The cold wall offered little comfort; instead, it felt like a prison, a barrier between him and the world he once knew. His face, streaked with tears, reflected a turmoil more profound than any child should have to endure. Each tear that fell seemed to carry with it the remnants of his lost innocence, pooling at his feet like the chaos that had invaded their lives.

When Kaelen entered the room, his heart sank at the sight of his son. Joren's flushed cheeks, damp from the emotional storm that had raged within him, were a stark reminder of the horror that had unfolded. He could almost feel the atmosphere crackle with the weight of sorrow, the unsaid words hanging heavily between them. The moment felt suspended in time, an inescapable reality that threatened to engulf them both.

Kaelen approached slowly, every step laden with the desire to comfort yet shadowed by a haunting vulnerability. He knelt beside Joren, the fabric of his worn jeans brushing against the cold ground as he leaned in to wrap his arms around his son. "Joren, listen to me," he murmured, trying to infuse his voice with a warmth that contrasted with the icy grip of fear that had settled in the room. "What happened wasn't your fault.

You did what you had to do to protect me." He could see the internal struggle reflected in Joren's wide, terrified eyes, the flicker of fear fighting against the flicker of understanding. Beneath that youthful brow lay a storm of confusion and guilt, raw emotions that twisted and turned, demanding to be acknowledged. Kaelen's heart ached at the thought of his son feeling responsible for taking a life, even in self-defence. How could a child carry such a hefty burden? The sheer weight of it made Kaelen's chest tighten, each breath a reminder of the injustice thrust upon Joren.

Kaelen brushed a thumb gently across Joren's tear-streaked cheek, whispering tender reassurances as if they were fragile threads that could weave some kind of solace. "I promise, we'll get through this together," he said, though he couldn't shake the gnawing doubt in his own mind. What if this moment transformed Joren in ways he couldn't yet comprehend? Would this trauma leave scars invisible to the eye but ever-present in his heart? Joren's gaze flickered to the shadows lingering in the doorway, an ephemeral reminder of the danger that now haunted their every step. The echo of that harrowing confrontation clawed at the edges of his consciousness, a relentless spectre that would not easily fade. Kaelen felt a surge of urgency wash over him. "We need to get going if I'm going to make it to work on time." He couldn't let dread paralyse them. They had to escape this suffocating space and push forward into an uncertain future. As he spoke, he searched Joren's face for any sign of hope, and for a fleeting moment, he saw it, a glimmer of the boy who had been fascinated by tales of spaceships and travels off-world, who had laughed uncontrollably at silly jokes. "Come on, buddy," he coaxed, his voice softened by the weight of resolve. "It will be okay. I'll be right by your side."

Slowly, almost painfully, Joren began to uncoil from his thoughts. He wiped his tears with the back of his hand, leaving behind a trail of glistening sorrow that highlighted the fragility of his spirit. With a deep breath, he straightened himself, though the tremor in his small frame lingered, a testament to the storm that still raged within.

Together, they ventured forth into the world outside, the air chilling against their skin as the haunting memories lingered like ghosts beside them. Kaelen felt a fierce protectiveness rise within him; he would not let this darkness define them. They had a journey ahead, a long road paved with uncertainty and healing, but Kaelen silently vowed to stand as a shield for his son, guiding him through the shadows, despite the haunting ghost of today. He held onto Joren's hand tightly, their fingers intertwined, a silent promise that no matter what lay ahead, they would face it together, step by careful step. They walked without speaking, as words failed them both. Eventually, they met their ally, a figure who had become a symbol of resilience in these shadowy streets, a man known as Eldric. The smog hung thick in the air, a suffocating veil that twisted the sunlight into a muted grey, making even the brightest corners of the city seem draped in despair. Joren leaned closer to his father, feeling both the weight of their predicament and the warmth of the bond they shared.

After Kaelen spoke a few private words to Eldric, a solemn expression crossed his father's face before he knelt to embrace his son. "Stay brave, my boy. I'll be back for you," he whispered, his voice barely cutting through the haze of uncertainty. With a heavy heart, Kaelen turned and walked away into the swirling murk, each step echoing the unspoken fears they both shared.

"It will all be just fine, young man," Eldric reassured Joren, a gentle smile breaking through the grime on his face like the rare glimmer of sunshine in a desolate afternoon. There was an air about him; his tattered cloak fluttered like a forgotten hero's banner, and in his eyes, Joren could see flickers of compassion intertwined with a steely resolve. "We have a clever plan to get you and your dad to safety, so don't worry about a thing!" Eldric's voice was steady, filling the boy with a hint of hope amidst the swirling darkness.

Under the jagged remnants of crumbling buildings, they made their way to a makeshift shelter. The faint glow of a flickering campfire danced in front of it, casting shadows that twisted like ghosts upon the walls of their makeshift sanctuary. Piled at one end were bags of recycled plastics, arranged into a makeshift bed that looked surprisingly welcoming, a stark contrast to the cold, sterile environment of the orphanage where Joren had spent his unhappy days.

"Here, eat this, and then you can get some sleep over there," Eldric said, handing Joren a mess tin filled with an unidentifiable stew. It smelled of herbs and smoke, a meal that should have repulsed him but, in that moment, felt like a feast. Joren accepted it without question, driven more by the need for sustenance than the thought of what he consumed. The flavours were muddled, but each bite warmed him from the inside.

Once he finished, Joren lay down on the makeshift bed, exhaustion pulling him into its embrace as quickly as the blankets enveloped him. He had barely closed his eyes before the weariness washed over him like a tide. Yet even as he sank into this strange realm of dreams, his mind was still racing. Here, under Eldric's watchful eye, he felt a flicker of safety, something he had not felt since the day he was thrust into the orphanage's cold, impersonal embrace. The beggar's kindness stood in stark contrast to the harshness of his past, igniting a small spark within him. For the first time, Joren allowed himself to consider the possibility that even in a world choked by despair and enveloped in a thick blanket of smog, heroes could still exist, perhaps not in the form he once imagined, but in the quiet strength and compassion of a stranger who seemed all too familiar. As he drifted off, he held onto that thought like a lifeline, realising that sometimes, kindness emerged from the most unexpected places, ready to guide the lost toward hope.

Nightmares twisted Joren's mind as monsters clawed at him in an overgrown wilderness. No one was around, and he felt overpowered when, suddenly, a dog leapt in from nowhere and chased the creatures away. The dog was hungry, so Joren fed him, and as a result, the nightmare subsided, allowing the boy to enjoy a much-needed peaceful slumber.

The night shift had settled into its usual rhythm for Kaelen, the familiar sound of cartwheels gliding along the tracks almost soothing against the metallic backdrop of the refinery. As he moved cart after cart of refined ore, he couldn't shake the feeling that this night was different. There was an undeniable tension in the air, thick with the anticipation of something unspoken. An increased quantity of ore had to be loaded for transport, and the train now boasted three extra carriages, a physical manifestation of the pressure mounting around him. It was a boon for their operations, allowing them to extend the train beyond the service tunnel's exit, giving them the cover they needed to reach the secret hold without raising any alarms.

Kaelen's thoughts inevitably drifted to his son, a small boy with an endless curiosity and an innate sense of wonder about the galaxy. It pained him to think of the risks he was taking, the choices that led him to this point. Was he doing the right thing for his family? The weight of doubt settled heavily in his chest. He remembered the dreams he had for the boy, dreams that seemed to slip further away with every dangerous decision. Yet the stakes felt impossibly high now; the ball had started rolling, and there was no turning back.

Upon leaving the refinery at the end of his shift, he encountered the watchful gaze of the security guard stationed at the gate. "Evening, Kaelen," the guard greeted, his voice gruff yet familiar. The guard glanced at the extra carts behind him, raising an eyebrow. "Looks like you had your hands full tonight. Big order from the Space Port Authority, eh?"

"Yeah, it's a hefty load," Kaelen replied, keeping his tone steady, though his heart raced at the implications of the rush order.

As he stepped out into the night, the distant wail of sirens cut through the stillness, echoing ominously through the chilly air. The sound seemed to drift in from the direction of the east canal, and for a moment, Kaelen stood frozen. Had the authorities found the body of Officer Lopez, whom he had carelessly disposed of? Unease clutched at his throat as he contemplated the implications.

"Another attack on a social engineer," the guard muttered as he walked up beside Kaelen, breaking through the haze of his thoughts. Leaning closer, he lowered his voice conspiratorially. "Those bastards deserve everything they get. No doubt some poor bugger will pay for this one, though. They always catch someone and make an example of them."

Kaelen felt his stomach knot. "Yeah, well, it's always the little guys who suffer," he replied, a bitter taste in his mouth. As the sirens continued to wail in the distance, he couldn't shake the feeling that his past decisions were inching closer to catching up with him, but he took a breath, said goodnight to the guard, and forced himself to move towards Joren.

The Train

Joren slowly awoke to the sight of his dad standing over him, a comforting figure bathed in the soft light filtering through the grimy window. The relief that washed over him was profound. It had been a harrowing journey, and he had nearly lost hope of ever seeing his father again. The trauma of the past weighed heavily on his soul, a dark cloud that seemed to follow him everywhere.

"Joren, wake up!" his dad called, his voice a mix of urgency and warmth. "We're going to head to the service tunnel soon, but first, we need to eat something. It's going to be a long journey ahead!" He handed Joren a mess tin filled with a substance that resembled porridge, its colour a pale beige. Joren took a cautious bite, and to his surprise, it was sweet and comforting, a brief reminder of more innocent days.

After finishing his meal, Joren felt a knot of anxiety tighten in his stomach, but he knew he needed to empty his bladder before they set off. He stepped outside, finding a secluded spot behind a crumbling wall, the cold morning air fresh against his skin. The world around him was quiet, the stillness broken only by the distant sound of rustling leaves.

Once he was done, he joined his dad, who was ready with a worn backpack slung over his shoulder. They exchanged a look of determination, both aware of the challenges they would face. The shadows of their past loomed large, but together, they were ready to confront whatever lay ahead. With a deep breath, Joren steeled himself for the journey, knowing that his father would be by his side every step of the way. They set off, leaving behind the remnants of what once was, venturing into the unknown together.

By the break in the rusted fence, Eldric handed two small, metal gas canisters to Kaelen. "Use them sparingly," he advised gravely, his voice barely above a whisper as if the words themselves might attract attention. "The train takes about four hours to pass through Dead Valley, and each canister holds roughly that much oxygen. You'll know when you're in the valley because the train will slow down, then speed up again as it exits. My advice is to hold off using the canisters until you start to feel it getting hard to breathe." He paused, scanning the surrounding area for any signs of trouble. "Oh, and one more thing," he added, leaning closer as if to share a secret. "The train will stop at an old, disused station on the other side of the border to unload the toxic materials it carries in the front carriages. When it stops, you need to climb out quickly, but be careful of the guards. They can be unpredictable. A contact will meet you there and help you navigate through the wasteland to the spaceport!" Kaelen nodded, absorbing the information. He felt a mix of gratitude and apprehension as he thanked Eldric for all his help. The air around them was thick with impending darkness, and as they approached the service tunnel, the smell of damp earth and rust filled his nostrils. Together, they climbed down into the gaping maw of the tunnel, the darkness enveloping them like a shroud as the sounds of the world above faded away.

The tunnel was damp, dark, and slippery, with the air heavy with the musty scent of mildew. It felt as though years of neglect clung to the stone walls, which were slick with moisture. Kaelen, having worked at the refinery for three years, had never encountered this forgotten passage. As they ventured deeper, the soft scurrying of small creatures echoed around them, sending a shiver down his spine. Flickering shadows danced in the dim light, enhanced by the faint glimmer of illumination at the tunnel's end. They squinted into the darkness, using the weak light to guide their steps. The light grew brighter as they approached, revealing a rusty ladder leading up to a manhole. With careful deliberation, Kaelen slid the heavy cover open, the metallic scraping breaking the oppressive silence of the tunnel.

The train was just a few meters away. Kaelen poked his head up from the ground, scanning the area for any guards or workers. To his relief, the coast was clear. He quickly climbed out and helped Joren up before silently replacing the manhole cover. The carriage they needed was two carriages ahead, so they moved carefully along and up against the side of the train until they reached it. Both of them slipped underneath, and as Kaelen opened the panel he had accessed before, he started to climb up when he discovered something that took him by surprise!

As Kaelen slipped into the dimly lit confines of the secret smugglers' hold, he carefully shone his torch around the narrow space. The beam cut through the darkness, revealing the shadows clinging to the rough, damp walls. The air was thick with the smell of metal and stale air. It was a cramped, foreboding place, and his gaze landed on a woman already hiding there. The eerie glow of the torch illuminated her pale, wiry frame, accentuating the sharp angles of her face. Her eyes, which looked like spent shell casings, were wide with surprise and fear as they met his. In her hand, she gripped a sonic-driver, instinctively pointing it at him as if trying to ward off a potential threat. Kaelen held his breath for a moment, assessing her. After what felt like an eternity, she lowered the weapon, realising he was neither a guard nor an engineer. As he climbed further into the cramped space, the dim light revealed more details: a small, worn leather jacket hugging her petite frame, with the faint outline of a tattered backpack slung over one shoulder. But it quickly became clear that she had no luggage at all.

His mind raced, spinning through a hundred scenarios as he took in every detail. She was small enough that there would be room for all three of them and his rucksack. However, he noted with concern that she wasn't carrying any supply of oxygen. The realisation hit him: if she decided to stay, he would have to share his own limited supply with her. That would be a gamble he was not sure he could afford. Yet, as he stood there, a flicker of hope ignited within him. His perception was that she was a decent person, likely in need of the escape just as much as he and Joren were. After taking a deep breath to steady himself, he helped his son Joren up and carefully resealed the panel behind them, feeling the weight of uncertainty settle in.

"It's going to be a difficult journey," he murmured, hoping to soothe his son's anxiety as much as his own.

Turning back to the woman, Kaelen offered a slight nod before introducing himself. "I'm Kaelen, and this is my son Joren," he whispered, his voice barely breaking the heavy silence. "I'm Nyx," the woman replied, her voice trembling slightly. The torchlight flickered across her features, capturing the scrapes and dirt etched into her skin, a testament to whatever peril had brought her this far.

"You know, Nyx, there is no oxygen to breathe when the train runs through the valley," he said, his tone serious. "I have some, and I will share it with you, but I can't guarantee that it will be enough; we're going to have to make it last!"

As the words left his mouth, her eyes widened, a mixture of surprise and gratitude washing over her face. Kaelen could sense the weight of her vulnerability and the shared desperation that connected them in this dark, confined space. In that moment, amid the uncertainty and danger, something unexpected began to bloom, an unspoken bond forming among them, woven together by their shared plight for survival.

As they waited for the train to start moving, Kaelen organised his rucksack to keep the oxygen canisters within easy reach. All three of them were lying on their backs, shoulder to shoulder, and Kaelen turned off his flashlight, explaining that he needed to preserve the battery power until they really needed it. As their eyes gradually adjusted to the darkness, he noticed it wasn't completely pitch black; small pinholes of light filtered in through holes in the sides and underneath the carriage, where a few rusted rivets had come loose. It wasn't enough light to work with the oxygen canisters, but it was sufficient to prevent a sense of panic about being trapped in the dark.

The Silent Journey

The moment the train roared to life, a sense of irreversible commitment gripped everyone's minds. There would be no getting off until the journey was complete, and there was a weight to that truth that seemed to settle over the passengers like a heavy blanket. As the train jolted forward, the sudden movement sent ripples of anxiety through the group. Above them, the iron ore shifted, causing the metal plates overhead to creak ominously under the pressure. Dust from the ore fell like fine snow, thickening the air and making it harder to breathe. Each breath felt gritty, as if they were swallowing the very essence of the industrial transport itself.

Kaelen pulled his son closer, wrapping his arm around the small figure to offer some sense of safety amidst the turmoil. Joren, with his youthful innocence, was acutely aware of everything around him. His senses, heightened by his Variant nature, were overwhelmed. The vibrations of the train felt like a living organism, thrumming with a chaotic symphony of clattering metal, clanking machinery, and the distant, eerie hum of energy that coursed through the very bones of the train. To Joren, it felt less like a means of transport and more like a tomb hurtling through an eternal abyss, closing in on him with every passing moment.

As he clutched a small, worn wooden toy spaceship, the last gift his sister had ever given him, the terror of their recent encounter loomed large in his mind. The memory of self-defence played on a loop, and he couldn't shake the fear of what they had done. The toy was a fragile connection to a happier time, and he held it tightly, using it as his anchor in the storm swirling in his thoughts. Though Kaelen's firm hold provided some reassurance, he, too, was battling his own demons. As they sped away from Neo-Veridia, the city they once called home slowly dwindled in the distance. The dense metal and iron ore surrounding them seemed to insulate them from the external world, no sounds of the crowded streets, no smells of the bustling marketplace, just the eerie sound of the train. In this unusual silence, Kaelen felt his senses heighten. The throbbing energy of the train pulsed through him, awakening abilities he had long thought dormant. Thoughts danced around him like whispers, and among them, he could even feel the fragmented thoughts of Nyx.

Nyx lay quietly next to him, her expression unreadable in the darkness, but her thoughts swirled with conflict. She was a woman of many layers, often shrouded in mystery, and at this moment, her mind raced with an array of emotions. The responsibilities weighed heavily on her shoulders; she felt the pressure of the decisions that had led her here. She was on the run, and the thought of what lay ahead left a pit of dread in her stomach. But there was also a glimmer of fury. She was determined to reclaim what was lost, even if it meant traversing the unknown dangers ahead. In this closed environment, Kaelen could almost sense the fierceness in her resolve, an electrical pulse that resonated with his own determination. He could feel Nyx grappling with her feelings of anger and regret, along with the flicker of hope buried deep within. They were together in this journey, facing the same darkness as shadows loomed and uncertainties took shape around them.

More than just the ability to read minds, Kaelen possessed a remarkable skill that allowed him to sense the ore above him with an acute awareness. As the train rattled along its tracks, he felt the ore shifting in response to the vibrations, as if it were alive. Each grain of ore revealed its unique characteristics to him; he could perceive the greater pressure exerted on the grains at the very bottom, while the upper layer was subject to the gentle caress of the wind that swept through the exposed carriage. Closing his eyes for a moment, he reached out with his mind, allowing himself to experience the ore as though he were physically holding it in his hands, feeling its weight and texture.

This exceptional sensitivity made him recognise what he was experiencing as telekinesis, a previously dormant ability. A thrill of excitement coursed through him as he contemplated the possibilities this ability offered. Driven by curiosity and determination, he decided to put his skills to the test. With intense focus, he zeroed in on one of the gas canisters, visualising it in his mind.

Summoning all his concentration, he nudged it with his thoughts, giving it a gentle shove. To his delight, he instantly heard the satisfying sound of the canister moving, its metal surface clanking against the other canister resting in his rucksack. The sound reassured him that he was on the right path and that his control over this newfound power was growing stronger. Kaelen couldn't help but smile at the prospect of what else he could accomplish with such extraordinary abilities, feeling both exhilarated and eager to explore the limits of his telekinesis as the train continued its journey.

The ride felt interminable, the sound of the train echoing in a relentless rhythm—cer-clunk, cer-clunk— as the carriage glided over the rail joints. Each time the metal wheels met the gaps, a jarring vibration surged through the floor, causing the entire carriage to shake for a fleeting moment. The noise, a mix of metallic scraping and the clattering of loose objects, created an unsettling soundtrack to their journey, amplifying the sense of confinement.

As the miles ticked by, the nervous energy of their predicament began to ebb, gradually replaced by an all-consuming discomfort in the cramped iron cage that held them. Crowded against each other, they shifted awkwardly, trying to find a more bearable position while the stale air hummed with tension. Despite the increasing unease, the flicker of hope for a better, safer life waiting at the end of the tracks kept their spirits from breaking completely. They exchanged furtive glances, silently encouraging one another, drawing strength from the belief that this journey would lead them to freedom and a new beginning.

Suddenly, there was a distinct change in momentum; the audible pattern from the rails shifted as the train began to slow down. "We must be reaching the valley!" announced Kaelen, pulling the cylinders from the rucksack. "I was told to hold off using these for as long as possible, so I think we need to remain calm and breathe as slowly as we can. As soon as we start to struggle, we will use them." Nyx and Joren nodded in agreement, and the three of them focused on slowing their breathing. While Nyx and Joren did their best to calm themselves, it was Kaelen who managed to maintain complete control, his nature shining through once again.

The train had slowed to a crawl, and a distinct change filled the air around them. It felt metallic and suffocating, even stinging their eyes slightly as it gradually replaced the air inside their desperate cabin. Nyx was the first to struggle, and Kaelen sensed this in her thoughts before she showed any external signs of distress. He turned on the torch, and as soon as his eyes adjusted, he handed Nyx a mask and opened the gas valve just enough to allow a trickle of air for her to breathe.

Shortly after, he sensed his son having the same difficulty, so he provided him with the mask from the other canister while maintaining his own breathing at a highly reduced rate. A few minutes later, he too needed oxygen. He tapped Nyx, who handed him the mask and held her breath. Kaelen took a large intake of oxygen and then passed the mask back to her. And that was how their ride continued.

Nyx made every effort to stay calm, forcing herself to slow her breathing even further as the metallic scent of the train rattled through the air. The rhythmic clanking of the rails echoed around her, each sound resonating deep within her chest. Kaelen, lying next to her, hardly disturbed the stillness; he required only one-fifth of the oxygen compared to everyone else, a fact that added an eerie calmness to his presence. The oxygen cylinder remained steady, its weight a reassuring anchor as they travelled through in darkness.

Joren, too, found his focus deepening. He concentrated on the subtle creaks of the train and the vibrations beneath him, matching the slow, reassuring clanks with gentle movements of his diaphragm. The stale air carried a mix of tension and anticipation, and he felt his heartbeat synchronise with the rhythm of the journey, grounding him in the midst of uncertainty. Each breath he took was deliberate, filling his lungs as he held onto the fragile sense of peace in an otherwise chaotic world.

They had been managing remarkably well for just under three and a half hours when the next bump in the road hit them. Nyx was taking a breath from the mask when the cylinder emitted a strange whistling noise, and Kaelen felt a surge of fear in his mind. He immediately turned on the torch again and forced his eyes to adjust. Looking at the gauge, he saw that the cylinder was empty! He glanced at Nyx and then at his son, weighing the risks he was willing to take with Joren's life. He made a crucial decision: he would not endanger his son, even if it meant that he and Nyx might not survive. He checked Joren's oxygen gauge and felt a wave of relief upon seeing that a third of the tank still remained. In an instant, he ran countless scenarios and calculations through his mind. He concluded two important things: first, they had already travelled most of the way through the valley, and the air should soon become breathable; second, if he could entrance Nyx with his mental abilities, he could slow her breathing enough to ensure that Joren's oxygen cylinder would last long enough for all three of them to make it through the remainder of their journey.

With that, he disconnected the line leading from Nyx's mask to the empty cylinder and, to her relief, connected it to Joren's.

Next, he used telepathy to speak to her: "Don't be afraid." This caused her eyes to widen, as having someone suddenly speak inside her mind was an unusual sensation. "I am a Variant, and I can use telepathy now that we are away from Neo-Veridia. I will help you relax and calm your breathing to make this oxygen last. I won't do anything to harm you, but if I don't do this, it simply won't be enough."

Nyx took a deep breath and nodded her permission. Kaelen then closed his eyes and focused intently, tuning into her thoughts, her panic, her heart, and her lungs. Bit by bit, he gently guided her into a deep sleep, so profound that she fell into a coma from which only he could awaken her. After that, he disconnected and signalled his son to use his mask, and that was how they managed to go on, father and son, taking turns while their fated companion slept soundly.

Every now and then, he turned on the torch to check the gauge, watching it gradually sink. He struggled with his protective instincts for his son as he wrestled with the idea of turning off Nyx's oxygen supply if it started to run too low. It was a difficult decision because he had promised her he would not do her any harm, but now the question of his son's survival was becoming paramount. With the gauge hovering just a millimetre above empty, he reached for the tap to turn off Nyx's supply. He hesitated for a moment, his thoughts battling fiercely within him. She wouldn't feel a thing, he reassured himself; she was so deep in a coma that it would be a merciful death for her, unlike his own, as he suffocated to let his son live. His son had to survive! His hand began to turn the tap, but then it happened. The pattern shifted again. The train was speeding up! He left the tap on and offered a silent prayer that they would be okay. After a moment, he inhaled sharply, only to cough at the metallic dryness of the air. Gritting his teeth, he collected himself and took another breath, then another. It was breathable; they had made it. Allowing a moment of relief to wash over him, he calmed his racing mind and focused on waking Nyx. Delving deep into her dreamy thoughts, he caught a glimpse of an image of himself as someone she quite favoured. It seemed that in their brief and confined time together, Nyx had developed romantic feelings for him. He felt a wave of embarrassment wash over him, but pushed those thoughts aside, concentrating instead on her heart and lungs, observing the subtle, steady breaths she was taking. Gradually, he increased the rhythm of her breaths, slowly coaxing her back to consciousness before finally releasing the connection.

As Nyx's eyes fluttered open, he felt a surge of joy, and he couldn't help but grin at her. She looked around, momentarily disoriented, but then her gaze settled on him, and the corners of her mouth lifted. A spark of recognition lit her eyes, and in that moment, they shared an understanding far deeper than words could express.

Once fully awake and out of the dangers of Dead Valley, their relief turned into an overwhelming wave of emotion. He edged toward her, and she met him halfway, the tension of the previous moments melting away. As they embraced, a celebratory smile broke across their faces. It was a moment filled with triumph and hope. They had not only survived but had also found solace in each other, a bond that now felt unbreakable. In that precious instant, the weight of the world felt lighter, and the three of them were ready to face whatever came next.

The Contact

It was time for the scheduled stop at the disused station of High Climb. Just as Eldric had advised, Kaelen carefully got out of the train, keeping an eye out for guards as he helped Nyx and then Joren out. The guards were up ahead, thankfully on the other side of the train, busy dumping their hazardous cargo over the edge of a steep slope. He waited patiently for the right moment, which came when one of the men began cursing after slipping and hurting himself, drawing the attention of all. He quickly signalled to Nyx and Joren, and the three of them slipped out from underneath the train and behind a wall of the old station.

As they crouched in the shadows, they could feel the oppressive heat of the sun building outside, a stark contrast to the chilly darkness beneath the train. Dusty sand dunes encroached upon the old station, creeping silently over the tracks and enveloping the forgotten structures. The desolate landscape stretched out before them, reminding Kaelen of why this place was often referred to as a wasteland. It felt fitting, given how nature had reclaimed the area, turning it into a graveyard of memories where laughter and movement were now just echoes in the wind.

Once the train departed, they were finally able to stand up, and they stepped into the brilliant sunlight, feeling the warmth wash over them like a gentle wave. This sunlight was different; it felt purer and more vivid than what they were used to in Neo-Veridia, where the sunlight had to battle through the thick smog and concrete-coloured haze that seemed to swallow so much of the world. Here, the light illuminated every grain of sand and every crevice of crumbling brick, filling the surroundings with a sense of raw, untamed beauty.

As they soaked in the brightness of their new environment, the tension in the air shifted. Soon, the train's rumbling engines faded into the distance, leaving nothing but a vast emptiness around them.

With smiles on their faces, they stood up and surveyed their surroundings, taking in the dry, parched land that sprawled out like an abandoned dream. "Eldric said a contact would meet us here!" Kaelen exclaimed, his voice breaking the stillness, filled with hope and determination as they prepared for what lay ahead. There was no sign of any contact, only a fallen signpost, half-buried in the sand. Nyx walked over to the signpost and pulled it out of the sand. The sign read, "Bermial 129 Miles!" "Well, at least we know how far we have to travel. It's just a shame we don't know which direction to go!" she said after reading it.

"Hang on a minute," Kaelen said as he dug away the sand with his hands, gradually exposing the base of the sign, "here, the base should match up with the sign!" And it did. Nyx held the sign in place, and they received their first clue.

Looking in the direction the signpost pointed, they could see nothing but open wasteland stretching to the horizon. However, to the east, a mountain range towered, which meant they could use the mountains as a fixed point to help guide them on the rest of their journey to the spaceport of Bermial.

Kaelen breathed in the fresh air and then spoke, "Well, I guess we better have something to eat and then get on our way, it will surely take us a couple of days to cover the distance ahead of us! Have you any food packed Nyx?", "Just some protein bars and a flask of water", she answered, "Same as us then!", he laughed to himself before adding, "I was so hoping you had brought a chocolate cake!" The three of them laughed as they all sat down and had something to eat.

"What was that!", asked Joren, looking at a low wall some thirty yards away, "What was what?", replied Nyx quickly turning around whilst taking the sonic-driver out of its holster ready to defend herself! "I don't know, I saw something move. Just for a second, it went behind that wall"

The three of them sat patiently, on high alert, just waiting for anything to happen. After a moment, they all noticed something move, or at least a shadow of something shifting behind the wall. Then, out popped a rather sad head. It was a dog that limped as it emerged from behind the wall, missing a front leg. The dog had a scruffy coat, dirt-streaked and matted in places, with a few patches of fur missing. A long scar ran across one flank, hinting at a painful past and adding to its weary demeanour.

It gingerly moved closer to them, its head held low and its large, brown eyes filled with sorrow and a quiet resilience. As it limped slowly nearer, it became clear that it did have a fourth leg, but it hadn't developed properly, remaining just a floppy mix of leg and paw dangling only an inch from its shoulder.

"She's hungry!" Joren said, feeling an immediate pang of sympathy for the dog, which looked as if it had endured a life as difficult as their own. "We can't give her food; we'll never get rid of her if we do!" warned Kaelen, his concern focused on the limited rations they already had for a two-day hike. "Aww, have a heart, Kaelen," Nyx said, smiling as she offered the dog a bit of her protein bar. Rolling his eyes, Kaelen retorted, "Well, you've done it now! I guess we have no choice but to take her with us!" Nyx smiled at him, knowing all along that he would have fed the dog even if she hadn't.

"Well, we can't just call her 'Dog'! What should we name her, Joren?" Nyx asked, still smiling as she rubbed the dog behind its ears. The dog leaned into her touch, seeming to find comfort in the gentle affection. Joren pondered for a moment, then moved to join Nyx in giving the dog some affectionate pats. Looking into the dog's warm, expressive eyes, he saw a life filled with hardship yet still burning with hope. "I think we should call her Echo!" he declared. As soon as he spoke the name, the dog barked happily, as if accepting her new identity. "Why that name?" Kaelen asked. "Because I feel she has had a difficult life, just like us; we are the same—she is our echo!" Joren explained. The dog barked again upon hearing the name. "Echo!" Kaelen called, and once more, the dog responded with a bark. "Well, she certainly likes her name. Well done, Joren!" said Nyx, her smile widening as she noticed the flicker of joy in the dog's eyes.

"We'd better get moving. We need to cover some ground before nightfall if we are going to manage with the supplies we have! " Suggested Kaelen. The group got up and started walking, and Echo, their new addition, happily limped along beside Joren.

Soon, they had walked so far that they could not see the station behind or much of anything in front of them, either, but the one constant that remained was the mountain range to the East, so they carried on, happy in the knowledge they were walking the right way.

Joren had never seen a spaceship for real, only heard stories of them travelling amongst the stars to faraway worlds. Other than in his own imagination, the closest he had ever got to a spaceship was the small wooden toy gift his sister, Elara, had given him. As they walked along, his mind was filled with thoughts of the many wonderful spaceships and other sights he would see at the space port when they arrived.

Nyx's mind was troubled by her affection for Kaelen. From the first moment she had seen him, not as a guard, and lowered her weapon back on the train, there was something about him that sparked a warm feeling in her heart. This warmth was something she thought would never return after the trauma she had experienced in Neo-Veridia.

Once, she had been a married woman, living in a lavish house with every comfort a person could desire, and married to a high-ranking clerk of the Authority. But that was before everything changed. She didn't come from wealth; rather, she had caught the eye of a hopeful young man who was well-off. He had dreamed of transforming Neo-Veridia into a paradise for both the poor and the wealthy. He advocated for this vision, and for the most part, his appeals were tolerated, as a necessary facade of concern was maintained for the less fortunate. By allowing his words to be heard, the Authority provided lip service to such arguments, thus preventing full-blown riots from the labourers who kept the city running. Only one of the Chief Directors, Judge Aemes, truly supported his ideals, but Judge Aemes was very old and his ability to wield power had grown weak.

Unfortunately, for Nyx's husband, one day, he pushed a little too far. His words struck too close to home for the High Chief of the city when he openly accused him of manipulating and enslaving Variants. He had revealed how the chief was holding their children to ransom in the city's inadequate orphanage. He had hit the nail on the head, but in doing so, had signed his own death warrant. That night, he allegedly slipped, hit his head, and was found floating lifelessly in the East Canal by

Officer Lopez, who was a Social Engineer. Nyx had never believed that version of events for a second; she was convinced that Officer Lopez was responsible for her husband's death. Following that, Nyx was evicted from her life of splendour and thrown out into the streets by Compliance Officers. She had ended up in a women's workhouse, washing the clothes of the wealthy in exchange for a bowl of porridge and a cold bed to sleep in. Yet now, she felt the kindness of Kaelen. Even during his mind control on the train, a part of him lingered with her. She sensed that he shared the same warmth her husband had shown, a warmth that suggested his life should have mattered more than it did. It seemed as if fate had brought them together from opposite sides of the same city. Now she smiled as she walked, happy to be in the company of Kaelen, Joren and Echo.

As dusk began to settle, Kaelen suggested that they make camp in one of the long-deserted, crumbling buildings they would every so often pass, so as the last few rays of light struggled on from the West, they sorted out a space to sleep in a half-collapsed home. Nights are cold out in the wasteland, temperatures often dropping below freezing, so they cuddled together as the chill began to creep in. Even Echo lay close to her new family, whilst she slept, keeping one ear upright, ready to hear any predatory noise. It was a shame Echo couldn't speak, for she knew too well of the terrors that

existed in the wasteland, in the cold of the night.
Terrors she wished to one day forget.

The hour had grown late, and a blanket of ice cloaked
the ground outside, making every sound sharp and clear.
Echo lay nestled among her pack, their rhythmic
breathing a comforting backdrop. But after five hours
of rest, an unsettling chorus began to emerge from the
East, creeping into her consciousness like a thief in the
night.

At first, the sounds were just whispers, faint and
distant, like the haunting memories of the wasteland she
held in the deepest part of her mind. But they grew
louder, wrapping around her like a cold embrace. As she
stirred, a sense of dread washed over her, flooding her
mind with those memories she had buried deep. She
recalled the chilling cries of lost companions, the
haunting howls of predators that lurked in the shadows.
Those sounds had once signalled danger, and now they
were returning to torment her.

Only Echo seemed to sense the urgency of the
moment. Lifting her ears, she strained to pinpoint the
source, feeling as if she were on the precipice of danger.
Her heart raced as she recognised the familiar sounds,
whistles in the wind that twisted memories of the past
into sharp reminders of her vulnerabilities. With each
note, fear gnawed at her gut, pulling her back to nights
spent alone in the wasteland, where survival meant
being constantly on guard. She kept her head low,
desperately hoping that whatever was out there would

pass them by, oblivious to her and the fragile pack she had come to cherish. They were her sanctuary, but the thought of their safety sent another wave of anxiety crashing through her. Then, as if to mirror her rising fears, new sounds emerged, unfamiliar and unsettling. Each crack and rustle sent her instincts into overdrive, awakening the primal part of her that knew all too well the perils of the wasteland. Those noises carried the weight of uncertainty, leaving Echo trapped between the solace of her current life and the haunting shadows of her past. As she listened, every muscle in her body tensed, her mind racing with images of what could come next. She had once been so alone, and now, she would do anything to protect her new family from the darkness that threatened to seep in once more.

The new sounds came from the engine of an armoured vehicle approaching them. It was the authorities, who had not only discovered the body of the social engineer in the canal but had also pieced together the puzzle surrounding the case. They knew that Kaelen was the last person to meet with the engineer that day and that no one had seen Kaelen or his son since the end of his shift. As a result, they ordered a search of the only train leaving Neo-Veridia since that time, which led them to find a hidden compartment and an empty gas canister on board. They had figured out how he had escaped, and now they intended to catch him before he crossed into Bermial, where they had no jurisdiction, and where he would become a free man.

As the soldiers neared, Echo growled quietly, disturbing her companions, who all immediately knew the authority was closing in on them. There was no way they could win in a fight, so they kept their heads down and kept hidden, and Nyx and Joren quietened Echo. Soon, the drone of the armoured car grew close, then slowly passed. But it then stopped, and everyone held their breath as they feared what would happen next. Nyx quietly removed her sonic-driver from its holster, her only weapon and greatly insufficient to counter an attack by a squad of the authorities' finest soldiers.

The door swung open, and a soldier dressed in full combat gear stepped out, his eyes focused on the ground. He appeared to be a tracker, searching for any signs or hints of tracks in the frozen tundra. "There's no sign of anything here, Chief," he reported.

From inside the vehicle, another voice called out, "Aye, it's a wild goose chase we're on!" After a moment's pause, the voice continued, "But a mission's a mission. Come on, lads, out with you all quickly! Search the buildings over to the right, just like we did with the others. If they're here, we will find them." With that, the tailgate of the vehicle opened, and four more men climbed out, heading towards the ruined buildings to conduct their search, while the chief remained in the vehicle, barking orders.

They knew it was only a matter of time before the soldiers found them, but they hoped against hope that they would give up and leave before extending their search any further.

As moments passed, the men searched, and the lights from their torches danced across the walls of the house, reflecting off various surfaces. Then, the chief shouted from the comfort of the vehicle, "Report in!"

"There's nothing here, Chief!" one soldier reported. "No sign of life anywhere," replied another, who was stood just yards away from where they were hiding. They knew that taking one more step closer would result in the soldier spotting them. The beam of his flashlight lingered in the room, moving slowly down the wall towards them. They huddled closer to the ground, trying to become invisible as the light edged nearer.

At that moment, Echo whimpered in fear, causing the soldier to stop dead in his tracks. He announced, "Hang on, I just heard something!" Another soldier responded, "So did I! It sounded like a whistling!" Just as he mentioned, the whistling noise, the air was suddenly filled with them, and everyone realised why Echo had been so afraid.

"AARRGHH…" one soldier yelled as he fired his weapon into the sky, only to be abruptly lifted off his feet and dragged upwards. The sound of his sonic driver was soon joined by the other soldiers, who were now also firing at phantoms in the sky. They were Night Beasts, formidable creatures from the shadowy mountains in the east, and their presence sent a shiver down the spines of the soldiers. With scales that glinted like obsidian in the faint light, they prowled deadly through the air, their every movement a haunting whistle in the night. Their eyes burned with an unnatural, fiery glow, piercing the darkness like twin torches, beckoning the unwary.

Each beast was a master of stealth and savagery, cloaked in a shroud of ancient magic and predatory prowess. Their elongated bodies, sleek and muscular, rippled with raw power as they stalked the soldiers.

The night air was thick with the scent of damp earth and the metallic tang of fear as they drew closer, their low growls reverberating through the stillness, a prelude to the chaos that was about to unfold.

One by one, they picked off the men with chilling precision, their claws slicing through the air with deadly grace. Muffled gasps and frantic cries filled the night as each soldier realised they were no longer in control. The once steady cadence of gunfire fell silent, replaced by the distorted screams of the last remaining soldier, echoing desperately in the dark.

As the soldiers fell, the Night Beasts feasted, their sharp teeth glistening with freshly spilt blood, a macabre testament to their insatiable hunger. The land seemed to pulse with their ferocity, the shadows dancing around as if celebrating the hunt. Those who witnessed the horrors knew that these creatures were not merely beasts; they were ruthless, furious killing machines, evoking fear akin to that of fire-breathing dragons swooping down from ancient legends, hungry and unrelenting...

The vehicle's engine roared to life, and it took off quickly, speeding along the frozen ground below. The group then heard whistling as the creatures tracked the vehicle. Suddenly, in the distance, there was a faint screeching of metal, followed by more gunfire. Afterwards, the sound of the engine faded, and the whistling ceased.

No one moved, no one spoke, and no one dared to make a sound—not even Echo. They all understood what had transpired: soldiers had been killed by some kind of winged beasts, and now they could only hope those creatures had moved on. Huddled together, they listened intently, fully aware of the need to watch for any signs or sounds. But nothing stirred in the frozen darkness, and after an hour, they began to relax and nod off to sleep.

Eventually, the entire group was asleep, except for Echo. Haunted by memories of her past encounters with the Night Beasts, which had left her with mental scars, as well as physical ones on her flank, she remained alert, guarding her newfound companions throughout the night.

The Space Port

Kaelen woke with a start, the vivid, violent sound of the Night Beast tearing through armour still echoing in his memory. The air in the ruined house was cold and still. The orange brilliance of sunlight in the wasteland filtered through the shattered windows and strained his eyes. He certainly was not used to waking to such brightness; it never happened back in the city, where the smog claimed most of the light.

Echo was curled tightly near the doorway, body tense, head resting on her front paw, but her eyes were open and fixed on the outside. She hadn't slept. He gently placed a hand on her head and whispered thanks, and with that, she closed her eyes and rested, knowing her guard duty was complete.

Joren was curled up in Nyx's arms as they both slept. Kaelen watched his son's chest rise and fall with each breath, feeling reassured that he was okay. The constant dull ache of fear for his son eased a little, and a smile grew on his face as he reflected on the revelations he had sensed about Nyx's feelings for him. She certainly had a special way with Joren, he thought, feeling his own heart open a bit wider. Looking away from Joren, he noticed that Nyx had opened her eyes and was smiling back at him with the same affection. The moment seemed to hold and last as their eyes met; it seemed like a perfect moment in time. Like a rare gift

amidst such chaos. Then life moved on a little as Joren
started to stir, and they broke their unspoken
connection.

"Good morning, young man," Nyx said gently to
Joren as he stirred in her arms. He opened his eyes and
replied, "Morning."

"It was a rough night, and I really don't want to
experience another one like that out here in the
wasteland," Kaelen started, "so, I propose we get
breakfast out of the way and then march as hard as we
can to reach Bermial before sundown!" Everyone
agreed with him.

Breakfast consisted of another protein bar and a
meagre drink of water. This time, Kaelen shared his
breakfast with Echo, grateful for her vigilance while
they slept. Afterwards, they stepped outside as the sun
rose, and the temperature began to climb rapidly,
melting the thin layer of ice that had coated the ground
overnight. The cold, brutal silence of the wasteland
returned, with the only sign of the night's slaughter
being the fresh, metallic scent of blood carried on the
dry air.

Leaving the ruined house that had provided them
shelter overnight, they found the sky clear now. The
predatory Night Beasts had long retreated to their
nesting grounds in the mountains to the east, far from
the light.

After walking for only half an hour, they found
themselves following faint tracks of disturbed earth,

presumably made by the Chief's armoured vehicle from the night before. Ten minutes later, Nyx spotted it: a bulky, black Grizzly-Class APC, a vehicle designed for urban control rather than desert patrol. "It's a wreck!" Joren exclaimed as he noticed the armoured roof peeled back in ragged strips.

As they approached the truck, Kaelen took a closer look. He couldn't believe the force those beasts must have used to shred the roof as if it were made from thin sheet metal. The interior of the vehicle lay in disarray, the echoes of chaos still palpable in the air. Shattered glass crunched beneath his feet as he stepped inside, the remnants of a once-sturdy window casting glimmers of light into the dim cabin. A chilling reminder of violence lingered as he used a rag to carefully wipe the blood from the driver's seat, the stark red a stark contrast against the worn, dark upholstery. As he settled into the driver's seat, his eyes were drawn to the dashboard, where he spotted the Authority identification chip of the deceased Chief, still firmly slotted in its place. With a swift motion, he pocketed the chip, convinced it might serve a purpose someday, even amidst the uncertainty. Darting his gaze around the engine compartment, he was relieved to see it largely unscathed, its metal surface gleaming despite the destruction surrounding it.

The thick, armoured tyres looked robust and ready to withstand any terrain. He took a deep breath, steeling himself for the task ahead.

As he began his assessment, his hands deftly moved over the various wires, coaxing them back into order. With focused determination, he bypassed and removed the Authority's location responder, knowing it would only serve as a beacon for unwanted attention. Finally, he turned his full attention to the engine, ready to coax it to life and escape the remnants of what had just transpired.

While he worked, Nyx wisely checked the storage compartments and bags in the back of the truck. There, she discovered extra rations: more protein bars, water, five empty oxygen cylinders, one full cylinder, and one half-full cylinder.

"I think we may have just saved ourselves a long walk!" Kaelen announced as he turned the key, and the large engine let out a guttural roar before coughing to life. Nyx hugged him and kissed him on the cheek. "Well done, you're brilliant!" she said. Joren and Echo climbed in, and soon they were driving the battered symbol of the Authority along a clear path. As Kaelen drove the APC, the barren wasteland gradually transformed into rolling fields, the dusty landscape giving way to vibrant greens that seemed almost surreal after their harrowing journey. His knuckles were white on the steering wheel, a testament to the tension coursing through him. He could feel the weight of the moment pressing down; every second felt like they were sprinting towards the edge of a precipice.

Beside him, Nyx sat with her heart racing, her wide eyes reflecting a mix of fear and exhilaration. For the first time in what felt like an eternity, she sensed that they were on the verge of something greater than mere survival. As she wrapped her arm around Joren to steady him in his seat, a fierce determination surged within her. She was where she was meant to be, fighting for those she loved. Each bump along the terrain sent jolts through her body, yet it reminded her that they were still alive, still moving forward.

Joren, though bruised and weary, found solace in Nyx's presence. His mind replayed their fractured journey, the close calls and moments of sheer terror. But as he felt her warmth beside him, a flicker of hope ignited within him. Despite the uncertainty of what lay ahead, he occasionally reached out to scratch Echo, whose nervous energy mirrored his own. The creature curled even lower to the floor, instinctively sensing the tension of their desperate flight.

Through the APC's broken windows, the fields stretched out like a promise. The vibrant landscape contrasted sharply with the darkness of their past, a stark reminder that they were fleeing for their lives. But with each passing moment, the horizon beckoned, and they could almost taste freedom, mingled with the bittersweet realisation that the end of their flight was drawing closer. Would it lead to safety or to confrontation? Each one of them clung to their thoughts, grappling with hope and dread as they sped towards an uncertain fate…

The distance soon faded as the giant engine roared across the flats toward salvation. As he drove, Kaelen pulled up the vehicle's navigation map. They discovered that the spaceport was more than just a place to board a ship; the map revealed it as a vast, multi-tiered installation. The first tier consisted of an industrial zone filled with warehouses, refineries, and, of course, a source of heavy toxic smog. Beyond that lay a security patrol road marking the boundary between the industrial nation of Neo-Veridia and the spaceport of Bermial. They had to find a way to cross that road undetected!

Kaelen knew he wouldn't be able to drive the APC all the way in; its ragged roof would make it stand out like a sore thumb. Meanwhile, Nyx studied the map, searching for a potential entry point. After some time, it appeared she had found one, possibly. The map indicated a security door on one side of the road, and she reasoned that if there was a door there, it might lead into the spaceport. It was guesswork, but at least they had a plan, a target to aim for.

They slowed to a normal speed as they approached a vast field filled with abandoned industrial debris, which appeared to be a dumping ground for outdated and obsolete machinery from the spaceport. According to the map, they were about one kilometre from the patrol road, but only half a kilometre from a bank of toxic smog. Kaelen pulled over, and they all gathered to examine the map, trying to figure out a route. There seemed to be no way to avoid the toxic smog, which stretched for about 300 meters in a low-lying valley they needed to cross. The map displayed imminent toxic warnings, and they knew they had to come up with a plan. Then Nyx remembered the oxygen canisters she had found. She moved to the back of the truck and returned with canisters and masks. Soon, they were all equipped with masks, supplying them with safe oxygen. Even Echo, who was now sitting on Nyx's lap, had a mask fitted onto her face with Joren holding it in place.

Kaelen manoeuvred the rig at a deliberate pace, intently studying the map and the jagged terrain that lay before him. The atmosphere thickened with a noxious haze, heavy with the chemical remnants of fusion reactor waste and propellant refining. Visibility diminished, but Kaelen skilfully guided the vehicle through the sprawling scrapyard and dumping zone, relying on his heightened senses to navigate the treacherous path more than his limited sight.

Nyx, full of confidence in his remarkable abilities, knew how extraordinary his instincts truly were. With patience and precision, they gradually emerged from the suffocating blanket of toxic smog, breathing in the fresh, invigorating air that followed.

Now positioned dangerously close to the patrol road, Kaelen took one last look at the faded map illuminated by the dim light of their flashlight. The distant hum of engines and the occasional crackle of radio chatter floated through the air, momentarily heightening their senses, but it proved to be nothing more than routine noise. simply the pulse of a world unaware of their presence.

With a steadying breath, Kaelen killed the engine, and they all slipped out of the vehicle, hearts pounding in their ears. Continuing cautiously on foot, the crunch of gravel beneath their boots was muffled by the sounds of vehicles driving past on the road and a spaceship landing with its thrusters firing hard. Shadows cloaked their movements as they weaved among the rusted remnants of scrap, each creak and rustle making them acutely aware of their surroundings and the necessity of remaining unseen.

Soon, they arrived at the security door, a heavy barrier looming before them. Its cold metal surface stood in stark contrast to the warmth of their anxious breaths. Beyond it lay their path to salvation, taunting them with promises of freedom just on the other side. But how could they open it?

With Nyx and Joren on the lookout for any patrols, Kaelen studied the lock mechanism, searching for a wire to short or a lever to pull. All he found was a slot. Desperation began to creep in, and in a moment of frustration, he kicked the door, catching Nyx's attention. She wrapped her arms around him in a reassuring hug.

"You can do this; I have faith in you!" she encouraged, kissing him on the cheek. Her words ignited something within him, and a memory flashed in his mind. He reached into his pocket and pulled out the Chief's ID chip. Holding it up, they both realised it was the perfect fit for the slot on the security mechanism control. "Should I?" he asked Nyx, who responded by interlacing her fingers with his free hand. Holding it tightly, she said, "Go on, try it."

Taking a deep breath, he inserted the chip, his heart racing with a mixture of hope and trepidation. A moment later, the mechanism sprang to life, and the locks clanked open. Kaelen pushed the door wide, revealing a dark tunnel that led beneath the road and into the spaceport.

In that moment, emotions surged within him, intertwining his fears about the uncertain future with the exhilaration of what lay ahead. As he turned back to Nyx, he saw the same thoughts reflected in her eyes, the same hopes, the same worries. But there was also a sense of determination that gave him courage. When she kissed him softly on the lips, it felt like a promise that whatever challenges awaited them, they would face them together. In that fleeting moment, despite the ambiguity of what the future held, it felt undeniably right.

Together, they would all step bravely into a future that awaited them.

<u>Epilogue</u>

We can all struggle when it comes to stepping into the future. It is only too convenient to turn away from the light and hide. We are not wrong for doing so, we are not unworthy for doing so. For the real truth is that we all have our own unique battles in life, and we should never make comparisons between them. Every step, no matter how small it may feel to you, is a win. And every journey starts with a single step, too. All we need to do is take enough of those little steps to reach our goals. Speed is not important, whilst taking the time to be kind to ourselves is.

Remember, you are the hero of your story, and I believe in you!

All the best, David Peters

DIVERGENT MIND BOOKS

If you enjoyed this book, why not read one of the following fantasy books:

Compilation – A Collection of Short Stories
By David Peters
Kindle Price £1.99   Paperback Price £8.99
ISBN: 978-1-7394124-7-0

The Miller's Apprentice
By David Peters
Paperback Price £8.99
ISBN: 978-1-7394124-8-7

The Life of Merlin
By Harriet Davey
Paperback Price £6.99
ISBN: 978-1-7394124-3-2

Alternatively, why not read the memoir:

BROKEN – A NEVER ENDING JOURNEY
By Louise Bourdon
Paperback Price £12.99
ISBN: 978-1-7394124-5-6

DIVERGENT MIND BOOKS ASSOCIATION

As an author, I've experienced the incredible power of storytelling. As someone diagnosed with autism later in life, I also understand the deep value of self-validation and having one's voice heard. This is why I publish my books with the valuable support of the Divergent Mind Books Association.

Their mission is to empower neurodivergent authors to share their stories with the world. They are doing this by providing low-cost ISBN numbers and free online courses to guide writers through their self-publishing journey.

Every book has the power to change a life. By supporting this association, you are helping to amplify neurodivergent voices, fostering a more inclusive society, and giving others the chance to achieve their goals and find their own sense of worth.

If you are interested, you can register for their free "Let's Write YOUR Book" online course.

For more information, please visit the Association's website at www.divergentmindbooks.org.uk